Summer Pony

By Jean Slaughter Doty

Illustrated by Ruth Sanderson

A STEPPING STONE BOOK™

Random House 🏠 New York

Text copyright © 1973 by Jean Slaughter Doty.
Illustrations copyright © 2008 by Ruth Sanderson.

RANDOM HOUSE and colophon are registered trademarks and A STEPPING STONE BOOK and colophon are trademarks of Random House, Inc.

www.steppingstonesbooks.com
www.randomhouse.com/kids

Educators and librarians, for a variety of teaching tools, visit us at
www.randomhouse.com/teachers

Library of Congress Cataloging-in-Publication Data
Doty, Jean Slaughter, 1924–1991
Summer pony / by Jean Slaughter Doty ; illustrated by Ruth Sanderson.
  p. cm.
SUMMARY: Disappointed with the half-starved and unkempt pony she has rented for the summer, Ginny hesitantly tries to help her.
ISBN 978-0-375-84709-7 (pbk.) — ISBN 978-0-375-94709-4 (lib. bdg.)
[1. Ponies—Fiction.] I. Sanderson, Ruth, ill. II. Title.
PZ10.3.D7197Su 2008
[Fic]—dc22
2006101902

Printed in the United States of America

24 23 22 21 20

Chapter One

It was a gloomy gray day in March. A threat of late snow was in the air when the station wagon bumped to a stop by the shabby barn.

Ginny was shivering. She got out of the car and waited for her mother. Somehow, everything here seemed awful and unreal. This was the day her dreams were supposed to come true. She was going to have a pony, a pony of her own, for the whole summer ahead.

Plans had already been made with the owner of the Sweetbriar Pony Farm. She could choose any one of all the ponies in his stable. But something was wrong. They must have made a wrong turn off the main road. Nobody could keep ponies in a place like this.

She could feel the cold mud oozing through her sneakers. Her mother came up beside her. She wore a hopeful look on her face. She was trying to make the best of a bad situation. "Here we are, dear. I wonder where Mr. Dobbs can be?"

The ponies of her dreams flashed through Ginny's mind. Which would she choose? A bright red-gold chestnut with a cream mane and tail? A black pony, with slim legs and a beautiful head like an Arabian? Or maybe a gray, the color of smoke? Shining coats and shining eyes, sleek and beautiful. They were waiting for her to choose—but not here. Certainly not here.

"Mother," Ginny whispered. "This can't be right. I never saw such an awful place." But Ginny knew, even as she stumbled after her mother. This was, indeed, the Sweetbriar Pony Farm. A faded sign saying so hung on the side of the sagging barn. Three little ponies stood in a nearby field behind a rusty wire fence. Their backs were humped up against the cold wind. A wheelbarrow with a broken handle was tipped over. It lay next to a soggy pile of manure close to the barn. There were hoof-prints everywhere in the mud around them.

A narrow door opened with a squeal of hinges. A tall, thin man came out. "Thought I heard a car," he said. "You must be Mrs. Anderson. Are you ready to choose a pony for the summer? Morning, miss. You must be the lucky little girl."

He stood back and waved toward the open door. "Come in. Come in and meet the ponies. Twenty of them, ma'am. All for you to choose from. Every one of them a pet. They're sound as a bell, safe for any child to ride and drive."

"Yuck!" said Ginny under her breath. She followed her mother through the narrow door into the dimness of the long barn.

Some daylight struggled through the dirty

windows. Two or three dim lightbulbs burned halfheartedly down the aisle. Here were no shining ponies waiting for her. No ponies turned their heads toward her as she came through the door. Instead, there were long rows of narrow stalls. The stalls were divided by broken boards. They were held together with pieces of wire. Inside stood odds and ends of ponies of all possible shapes and sizes. Most of them were very small. All of them were thin and shabby.

"My daughter has not had much riding experience," Ginny heard her mother say. "Just a few years away at a camp where they taught riding once a week. But she has always dreamed of having a pony of her own. So instead of sending her back to camp, we thought we would rent a pony for the summer. We'll keep it at home—as a birthday present. . . ."

Mr. Dobbs mumbled an answer, but Ginny didn't hear. She moved down the narrow aisle between the stalls. She looked in shock at the ponies on either side.

"You poor little things," Ginny whispered. The ponies turned their heads to watch her. The air was stale and sour and heavy. It smelled of dirty ponies and dirty stalls. Ginny wanted to cry. She wanted to run outside and forget this awful place. She wanted to go and find the white-fenced pony farm that she had pictured. It must exist somewhere, and there her dream ponies must be waiting.

But she knew at the same time that only this was real. Her parents had said plans had been made. Someone had suggested Mr. Dobbs. How could this be? So her mother and father, who knew nothing about horses and ponies, had somehow found the Sweetbriar Pony Farm. She had to choose a pony here. Or no pony . . . anywhere . . . at all.

Ginny took a long, shaky breath. She went on down the aisle. Most of the ponies were little Shetlands. They were much too small to carry her. She could make out a taller chestnut with a white blaze on his face. He was big enough to carry her. She stopped hopefully near his stall. She admired the pony's beautiful head and large, dark eyes.

Mr. Dobbs came hurrying up beside her. "I don't think this one will do, miss. He's a young stallion. He's a little spirited for a new rider." Ginny drew back. The chestnut flattened his ears against his head. Then he snapped at Mr. Dobbs with his lips drawn back. His teeth were showing.

"That one would take your arm off," muttered Mr. Dobbs. "Don't know why I keep him. But I love them all, you know." He smiled at Ginny's mother. Ginny walked away angrily. If he loved his ponies all that much, why didn't he take better care of them?

There was one other pony down at the far end of the barn. Ginny could just barely see it, but it at least looked tall enough for her. Mr.

Dobbs dashed past her with a rope in his hand. "I'll show you a good one," he said. "This is the best in the barn. Very gentle," he said to Ginny's mother. She was still looking a little shaken by the bad-tempered chestnut. "And this one is just the right size for your little girl." He rushed into the stall and backed the pony out.

Ginny's heart sank. This was her last chance. It was the only other pony of the right size left in this awful barn. It was a sad sight. The pony was so many colors that Ginny couldn't make out what they all were. Ginny was disappointed.

Mr. Dobbs shoved a bridle on the pony's head and led it outside. It was a mare, Ginny discovered. Under the dirt and grime she was white with large patches of dark brown spots. Her tail was black. Her mane was white. And the forelock that almost covered her eyes was as black as her tail. Ginny went up to the pony. She offered her a lump of sugar from the pocket of her blue jeans. The pony took it and ate it slowly. Then she turned her head to look at the little Shetlands in the field behind the fence.

"Why, she's blind in one eye!" gasped Ginny.

"No, miss, she's not blind. She's got one brown eye and one blue one. Just because they don't match doesn't mean she can't see perfectly well. Makes her look a bit special, don't you think? Come on, then, up you go!" Before Ginny knew what was happening, he had boosted her up onto the pony's thin bare back. He put the reins into her hands. "Off you go and give her a try. Enjoy yourself."

Ginny glanced at her mother. She was smiling. "You look very nice on her, dear," she said. Ginny smiled back. But her face felt stiff, as though the smile would crack it. She turned her attention to the thin pony under her. "Come on, you poor creature," she said under her breath. "Let's get this over with."

* * *

They slopped through the mud. They found firmer ground over by the edge of the field. It had been ages since Ginny had last ridden— not since last September. That suddenly seemed a long time ago. She had never been allowed to ride without a saddle at camp. The pony felt very different and bony and strange under her. She took a handful of the pony's white mane in one hand and squeezed with her legs.

The pony started to trot. Ginny was surprised. The trot was smooth. She was having no trouble staying on. She pulled on the reins. Right away the pony came back to a walk. Then Ginny asked her to canter. The dead wet grass squelched under the pony's hooves. She cantered slowly beside the wire fence. Ginny slid a little from side to side, but finally found her balance in the middle. She pulled the pony back to a walk and turned her. She cantered back to her mother and Mr. Dobbs. They were waiting by the barn door.

"Lovely, dear," said her mother.

"Nice little mare," said Mr. Dobbs.

The spotted pony stood still, with her head down. She was as worn out as if she'd gone on an hour's hard ride. It had finally started to snow. Ginny could see the flakes melting in the pony's dirty mane. She could feel her own soggy braids. They dripped down her shoulders and soaked through her jacket.

There was a silence. Both her mother and Mr. Dobbs were looking at Ginny and waiting. In spite of all the dampness, Ginny's mouth felt dry. She discovered in one quick moment that disappointment seemed to have a funny taste.

"She is a nice pony, Mr. Dobbs," Ginny said at last. "She'll be just perfect." She slid off the pony's back without looking and landed in icy mud up to her ankles.

Mr. Dobbs beamed. "A little spring grass will have her fattened up in no time," he said cheerfully. "Hay gets poor at this time of year." Ginny turned away. She was afraid her dislike showed in her face. She knew there was no excuse for the ponies to look so thin and unhappy. It didn't matter what time of year it was.

Mr. Dobbs led the pony back into the barn.

Ginny stood and watched the pony go. The pony's sharp hip bones stuck out. Her drooping black tail hung down full of mud and burrs.

"There you go, dream pony," she said to herself. "But at least I'll just have you for the summer. I'm not stuck with you forever. And you are a whole lot better than no pony at all."

Chapter Two

The morning sunlight shone through the window onto Ginny's face. Only half awake, she buried her face in the pillow. She pushed her feet down to a cooler spot between the sheets. Morning. Wednesday. Wednesday morning. She sat up, suddenly wide awake. Today was the day the pony was coming.

Ginny looked across the room at her shelves. They were jammed with stories about horses and ponies and books on how to ride and care for them. On the top shelf her collection of glass and china horses sparkled in the sunlight.

Ginny grinned as she swung out of bed. It

was a good thing she'd dusted her tiny horses just a few days ago. They would not get the attention this summer they had always been given before. They would have to wait on the white shelf. The summer pony was ugly and shabby. But at least she was real.

Everything was ready. Ginny's father complained because he would have to leave his car outside all summer. Yet he had cheerfully built a temporary stall for the pony at the back of the garage, near a window. Ginny still shuddered at the memory of the dark, airless barn where they had found the pony on that dreary day in March.

But that had been a month ago. Now the grass was starting to turn green. There were small, sprouting leaves on the trees. The days were getting longer. Summer was almost here.

Two clean, new metal garbage cans stood in the garage. They had tight-fitting lids to keep field mice out. They were filled with oats and a mixture of grains. The feed dealer had called it "sweet feed." He promised it would "fatten up a fence rail."

There were six bales of hay and five bales of straw. One bale of straw had already been opened. It was spread into a deep, golden bed in the stall. There was a heavy black rubber feed tub hanging in one corner of the stall. There was a bucket for water in another corner. A brick of salt in a holder had been nailed to the wall near the feed tub. A box of brushes stood on a shelf near the window. Inside were a mane comb and hoof pick.

Everything was ready and waiting—but there was still school today. Ginny groaned. The pony wouldn't be delivered until late afternoon, well after school was over for the day. There was really nothing more to do but wait.

Riding on the school bus, then sitting through her classes, Ginny's thoughts swung between excitement and despair. The pony was an awful-looking thing. But her shabby winter coat would finish shedding out. She'd have some proper food and good care. Then maybe she would look a little better.

Ginny wished she could talk to someone about it. But none of her classmates had the least interest in anything to do with horses. Ginny drew a row of pony heads down the margin of her math paper. The spotted pony would never look like Pam Jennings's pony, of course. Pam's pony was beautiful. It was half Thoroughbred and half Welsh. It was the color of a new copper penny. And it had won a ton of ribbons and championships everywhere. . . .

Ginny shut her eyes. She tried to squeeze the thought of this pony from her head. She'd heard Pam was a stuck-up thing, anyway. So who cared? They were the same age. They lived quite near each other. But the two girls went to different schools and had never met. Ginny had seen Pam and her pony at a number of local shows. That was the kind of pony that she had wanted for herself this summer, Ginny admitted gloomily.

Ginny stared down at the paper on her desk. She saw that she'd drawn the pony heads in the margin with ink. She'd never be able to erase them. With a bored sigh, she began to copy her math problems on a fresh sheet of paper. She chewed thoughtfully on the end of one braid and stared blankly out of the school-room window. She felt sure the morning would never end.

The school bus finally brought her home. Four o'clock came, and then five. Mr. Dobbs was late. Ginny's mother was talking about starting dinner. Daddy would be home soon. Had Ginny set the table? But Ginny barely heard and paid no attention. She felt as though her ears had grown stiff from listening for the sound of truck wheels on the driveway.

Ginny and her mother heard it at the

same moment. The clashing of gears. The rattling of a tired engine. The sound of tires on the drive. They flew out the back door. A battered green pickup truck, with high board sides, stopped outside the garage.

"Evening, Mrs. Anderson. Got your pony here, safe and sound." Mr. Dobbs went to the back of the truck. He opened it and disappeared inside. Ginny could barely breathe. She heard thumping sounds. Mr. Dobbs called out, "Whoa!" in a loud voice.

Suddenly the pony's head showed at the back of the truck. Mr. Dobbs shouted, "Whoa!" again. But the pony paid no attention. Her eyes were on the green grass growing close to the driveway. She took one eager sliding step and jumped out of the truck.

She was thin and hungry, weak and shaky from the ride in the strange truck. The pony stumbled as she landed. Her knees buckled, and she fell. She began to eat while she was lying there on the grass. She didn't even pick up her head.

Ginny and her mother stood frozen with shock. They stared at the tired, hungry pony. She was lying in a heap on their lawn. Mr. Dobbs was embarrassed. He rushed to the pony's head and tugged at her halter. With a tired sigh, she got slowly to her feet.

"There we are!" cried Mr. Dobbs. He thrust the pony's frayed lead rope into Ginny's hand. Ginny just managed a stiff, polite smile. Mr. Dobbs took a folded check from Ginny's mother and buttoned it carefully in the pocket of his shirt.

He drove off quickly in his clattering truck. *He's afraid we might change our minds,* Ginny thought bitterly. She and her mother looked in silence at the thin, shabby pony. She was standing patiently in the driveway. Her brown ears were pricked. Her messy black forelock was falling over her mismatched eyes.

"How nice to have a pony here at last," said Mrs. Anderson.

"Wonderful," said Ginny. She hoped that she sounded more cheerful than she really felt inside. "Gosh, I forgot to ask Mr. Dobbs what her name is. Come on, old girl." She led the tired pony into her new stall.

"Perhaps you could name her Patches?" suggested Mrs. Anderson that evening after dinner. Ginny leaned over the side of the stall. She gazed at the pony thoughtfully. She noticed that the pony had finished all her hay and had started to eat her straw bed.

"Do you mean that moke belongs to us?" Ginny's father was being shown the pony for the first time. He sounded like he was trying not to laugh.

"She doesn't belong to us," Ginny said quickly. "She's only here for the summer. And what is a moke, anyway?" She wanted to distract her father before he laughed out loud.

She didn't really care what a moke was. But she knew the best way to change any subject with a grown-up was to ask a question.

Mr. Anderson started to fill his pipe. "When I was a boy, I had a friend who came from England. He used to tell us about a donkey he had at home. He called it a moke. Great word. Moke. I always liked it." He studied the pony. "Does it eat like that all the time? Or does it stop sometimes to rest?"

Ginny was grateful for the soft light over the stall. The pony's ribs and hip bones didn't show up as clearly as they did in daylight. She had to agree the pony wasn't much to look at. It wasn't the pony's fault, though. Ginny didn't think she could bear it if anyone laughed at her now.

Ginny was tired and confused. Yet it really was wonderful having a pony, even this one. She picked up a fresh armful of hay. She piled it in the corner of the stall. "Here, you silly old moke," she said in a shaky voice. "This is better for you to eat than straw."

Ginny's father gave her a quick hug. "Go to bed. You're asleep on your feet. Your moke will still be here in the morning."

Chapter Three

It was barely daylight the next morning when Ginny slipped out of bed. She tiptoed quietly downstairs in her bathrobe and slippers. She took a carrot from the refrigerator and went out to the garage.

The pony was really there. She turned her head toward Ginny and nickered softly in a gentle sound of welcome. Ginny tried not to feel pleased. She knew the pony was just asking to be fed. But it felt nice to be greeted so warmly, anyway. She gave the carrot to the pony and patted her on her shaggy neck.

Everything smelled so good. The whole garage smelled of fresh spring morning. It smelled of the new wood of the stall. And of hay, and feed, and pony. Ginny shut her eyes. She drew in a long, deep breath. There was no question about it. This just had to be the most wonderful smell in the world.

The pony banged her hoof eagerly against the stall door. Ginny laughed. She hurried to fill a small wooden measure with oats and sweet feed. She poured it into the feed tub in the stall. Then she watched as the pony gave a sigh of pleasure and started to eat.

One quart of grain didn't look like much to Ginny. But the manager of the feed store had warned her to be careful. "If this pony of yours is as thin as you tell me," he had said, "you can be sure she hasn't seen a grain of oats in a long time. If you take a pony in that shape and throw the good feed into her, you'll kill her for sure. What they call killing by kindness. Good hay won't hurt her, and all the fresh, clean water she'll drink. But take it easy with the grain."

The pony chased the last oat around the bottom of the feed tub and ate it. Then she waited while Ginny brought her an armload of hay.

It took forty-five minutes for Ginny to put the bridle on the pony later that morning. Ginny struggled with the tangle of straps and bit. It had looked like a bridle when Mr. Dobbs had handed it to her the evening before. But then she had lifted it down from its hook that morning. Somehow it had become a jumbled handful of leather and buckles.

Ginny had bridled one or two horses at camp before, but only with a counselor standing beside her. The bridle had been given to her in proper order. The reins were just so. The headpiece was in one hand and the bit hung neatly where it belonged. Everything was different now that she was alone.

Annoyed with herself, Ginny finally sat on a bale of hay. She put the bridle down and fixed the jumble of leather. Once she had it looking like a bridle again, she remembered how to slip the bit into the waiting pony's mouth. She put the headpiece over her ears. Flushed with pride, she buckled the throat-latch. Then she led the pony out of the stall.

Her father and mother were waiting to see her off on her first ride. "Don't you have a saddle for the moke?" asked Mr. Anderson. Ginny wiggled up onto the pony's bare back.

"I didn't see one, so I guess not," said Ginny. "Unless Mr. Dobbs gave it to Mother when I was holding the pony yesterday." But her mother shook her head. "I can't see what possible difference it could make, anyway," said Ginny. "The pony's not about to buck me off or run away with me. I don't think she has that much energy."

"Ginny's probably right," said Mrs. Anderson. "We can always get one later on if she needs one, I suppose."

Mr. Anderson gave the pony a friendly

slap on her shaggy rump. "On your way, then. Have a good ride, you two."

Ginny shortened her reins nervously. She squeezed the pony with her legs. Much to her relief, the pony swung off at a willing walk. Her head was up. Her ears were pricked cheerfully. Ginny didn't dare take one hand off the reins to wave. She smiled stiffly over her shoulder at her parents instead. Then she turned and rode the pony down the drive.

The pony stopped right away at the road to let a car go by. Then she walked on promptly when she was asked. Ginny began to relax. She was even able to laugh at herself when she saw how tightly her hands had been gripping the reins. In a short time they were in the woods. The paths Ginny had walked so often in the past opened suddenly into a fresh and wonderful world.

Everything looked completely new and different from the back of the pony. There was cheerful activity in the woods that Ginny had never noticed before. The squirrels and chipmunks went about their busy lives. They were not disturbed by the muffled sound of the pony's hooves on the loamy paths.

Ginny was glad to see a doe with her young, wobbling fawn. They stood in a sunny clearing. They did not turn away when the pony saw them and stopped. The doe and the pony looked at each other, unafraid. Ginny sat absolutely still. She hardly dared to breathe. She didn't want to make a movement that might startle the deer. Finally the doe turned her lovely head to nuzzle her fawn. She led it into the deeper shadows of the woods without making a sound.

Ginny and the pony came to the stream that crossed the path. Ginny let the pony stop in the middle to drink. The pony took a few swallows. Then she began pawing the water. Ginny clutched at the reins with alarm. Then she realized with amusement that the pony was just playing with the water. The pony liked the splashing sound and the sprays of water flying from her pawing hoof.

Suddenly the pony's knees buckled. The next thing Ginny knew, she was standing in the middle of the stream. The icy water was halfway up to her knees. The reins were still in one hand. The pony was lying in the water beside her. She was clearly enjoying herself.

Ginny squished over to a rock beside the stream. She put her head in her hands. Then

she laughed until she cried. Finally she stood up. She pushed her braids back over her shoulder. She wiped her eyes. And she gave the reins a strong tug. The pony blinked and scrambled to her feet. She shook herself like a dog and sprayed water in all directions.

"That was silly!" gasped Ginny. She was laughing and shivering. She tried to dodge out of the way of the drops of water. "Cut that out, you idiot pony! That water is cold." She flung

herself onto the pony's wet back. She urged her into a brisk trot, then into a canter. They burst out of the woods into the warmer sunlight of an open field. Ginny was still laughing. She pulled the pony back to a walk. Then she patted her on the neck.

They walked and dried out in the sun. A few minutes later, Ginny realized that she wasn't nervous anymore. She had forgotten to worry about her riding. She would get along very well. If she remembered to keep the pony moving when they crossed a stream, she told herself with a grin.

Ginny and the pony drifted across the field. They were enjoying the warmth of the spring sun. The whole golden summer stretched ahead. Ginny was a little bit stiff and sore, but she felt calm and happy. She turned her pony's head toward home.

Chapter Four

It took three soapy baths in a row, and many heavy buckets of warm water, to get the pony clean. On the first warm Saturday morning, Ginny carried the buckets down the kitchen steps. The pony was tied under the flowering branches of a small apple tree. Ginny rubbed the suds into the pony's coat and mane and tail. Then she rinsed her off and washed her again. Ginny was soaking wet. Her shirt and blue jeans and sneakers were splashed with suds and water. But she didn't mind.

The pony looked much better as she stood dripping in the sun. A lot of her shaggy winter coat had come out with the scrubbing. Her white markings were now spotless. The brown patches were beginning to shine a warm chocolate color as she dried.

Ginny sat down to catch her breath on the bottom kitchen step. But she jumped to her feet a moment later. She was startled to hear someone calling her name. "Ginny? Hi! My name is Pam Jennings. Our place isn't very far from here. Did you know we're almost neighbors? May I see your new pony?"

And it really was Pam Jennings coming around the corner of the house. She was holding an apple in her hand.

Ginny would have known Pam anywhere from watching her ride her beautiful pony at so many shows. "Hi. Oh, gosh, I'm a mess. I'm Ginny Anderson. How nice of you to come." Ginny stumbled over the words. "The pony's not really mine. I just have her for the summer. She's kind of a mess, too, right now. I've just given her a bath."

"She looks lovely." The dark-haired girl

held the apple out to the pony. The pony bit into it gently. "She has nice manners. Are you planning to show her this summer?"

Ginny just shook her head silently. Wild pictures raced through her mind. She saw rows of elegant show ponies in a ring. Everyone was laughing at her thin, shabby, strangely marked pony beside them.

"That's too bad." Pam stroked the pony's wet head. "It would be fun to have someone to go with. But at least we can ride together, can't we? There's no one nearby who has a pony. I was so glad when the feed man told Michael there was finally another pony in the neighborhood." She rubbed the pony's wet ears. "Michael takes care of Firefly, my pony. And of my mother's and father's horses." Ginny had no idea what to say, so she just nodded.

"What do you call her?" asked Pam.

"Her name is Mokey." There. It was said, out loud. The nickname had stuck. For days, everyone in the family had called the pony "the moke." Then, one day, she was Mokey.

Pam gave the wet pony a final pat on the shoulder. "Good-bye, Mokey. I have to go now. Mother is waiting in the car. Do you want to meet tomorrow morning at my place for a ride, Ginny? About eleven o'clock?"

"Okay," Ginny said faintly. Pam hurried away. Ginny fell again onto the bottom of the kitchen steps. She had her chin in her hands. She stared at her spotted pony half asleep under the tree.

"It will be a lot of fun," she said to herself firmly. "But oh, dear, Mokey, I wish you were just a little bit more elegant." She made a face at the idea of Mokey plodding along behind the graceful Firefly. Pam would be riding so beautifully in her well-cut breeches and shining brown boots, while Ginny rode bareback in blue jeans and sneakers.

At the same time, Ginny knew she was being unfair. Pam really had seemed very nice.

Ginny loved riding alone with Moke. But it would be nice to have company once in a while to share some of the fun. She got up and unclipped the rope from Mokey's halter. Then she turned Mokey loose to graze on the lawn.

"But don't you lie down and roll and get yourself dirty," Ginny told the pony. "You may not be beautiful, but at least you can be clean."

Mokey did roll, of course. She loved the feeling of the sun-warmed grass on her drying coat. She got up and shook herself proudly. She had grass stains all over the white parts of her coat. There were also some in her mane. She needed another bath. The backyard looked like a battlefield when they were finished. The lawn under the apple tree was a small sea of soapsuds. Great chunks of earth had been scooped up out of the lawn where the pony had rolled and dug her hooves into the ground.

Ginny walked Mokey dry. She tied her up in her stall. Then she looked at the torn-up lawn gloomily. This was going to be one of those days she would be glad to see end.

Of course Ginny's father was mad about the holes in the lawn. Her mother was annoyed at the splashes of soapy water on the kitchen floor. As soon as she could, Ginny bridled her pony and set off down the driveway at a brisk trot. Mokey swung along cheerfully. Her head was up and her ears were pricked. She was as glad as Ginny to be out for a ride.

When they got home, Ginny slid off Mokey's back. Her father was waiting and smoking his pipe. Ginny was glad to see that he looked much more cheerful than he had earlier, rolling the lumps out of the lawn.

Ginny brushed the mud and dust off Mokey's legs. Her father was holding the pony's reins. Ginny noticed with surprise that he was patting Mokey's neck.

"I thought you said you didn't like horses," said Ginny with a smile.

Mokey nudged Mr. Anderson's arm with her soft muzzle. He began to rub her behind the ears in her favorite spot. "I don't like horses and ponies in general. But I think I like this one," said Mr. Anderson. "And I'm glad you're having such a good time with her. But, Ginny, keep her off the lawn! You know that big oak tree down the hill beyond the house, just where the lawn ends? Why can't you tie her to that tree with a rope? You can let her eat the long grass down there."

"I think that's a wonderful idea," said Ginny. Her father got a rope from the garage. The two of them led the pony down the hill. They tied one end of the rope to her halter. They tied the other end around the trunk of the tree. The grass was lush and tall. Mokey started grazing happily.

Ginny and her father walked back up toward the house. They turned for a moment to enjoy the sight of the pony. She was calm and happy. She grazed quietly under the tree.

Suddenly Mokey seemed to go crazy. She flung herself into the air on her hind legs. Then she crashed to the ground. She staggered to her feet. Then she fell again. Ginny started to run toward her as fast as she could.

She didn't hear her father shouting or his footsteps running to catch up with her. She reached the thrashing pony. But her father's strong hand on her shoulder threw her backward. She tripped and fell. "Let me go!" she yelled at her father. "Something awful's the matter with Mokey!"

"Stay away from that pony!" her father shouted. "Stop it, Ginny! You can't go near her now! She's in such a panic. She'll kick you to pieces!" Ginny struggled to her feet. She stood still for a moment. She was gasping for breath. They could see now what had happened. The pony had moved at the end of the long rope and the rope had twisted around her hind legs.

It had scared her into a panic. She had fought the rope wildly. Then she had been thrown down on the ground. She was foaming with sweat from fear and tiredness.

Now the pony was lying still. Only her sides were heaving. She gasped for air. "Move quietly," Ginny's father said in a low voice. "I don't know much about horses. But panic is pretty much the same in any living thing. Go to her head, Ginny. Stay out of the way of her hooves. Talk to her. See if you can keep her quiet. I'll get a knife to cut the rope."

Ginny knelt in the grass by the pony's head. Ginny's common sense was slowly coming back. She knew her father was right. She was ready to jump to her feet and out of the way if the scared pony started to fight again.

But Mokey seemed almost unconscious. Her eyes were glazed. Her breath rasped in her throat. She didn't try to move even when Ginny's father came back. He started to cut the tangled rope with a sharp knife.

The rope finally lay in pieces on the ground. "Why doesn't she get up?" said Ginny. Her voice was shaking. "She's free now, but she doesn't seem to know it!"

Mr. Anderson pulled a last piece of rope away from the pony's front leg. "I wonder if she's in some kind of shock," he said. "Ginny, talk to her. Try to make her get up."

"Maybe her legs are broken," sobbed Ginny. The tears she had been holding back poured down her cheeks at last. "I've never seen anything so awful in my life! Get up, Mokey, get up!"

But the pony just lay flat on her side. Her legs were limp. Her head stretched out on the ground. Ginny became dimly aware that her mother was standing beside her. "I saw it from the house," she said. "John, do you think the pony could have broken her back?"

"If she hasn't, we're lucky," Mr. Anderson said. "Come on, old girl. Try to get up." He gave the pony's halter a gentle pull.

Mokey moved. She blinked. She lifted her head. Slowly and with great effort, she put out one foreleg. Then another. "That's it! Good!" said Mr. Anderson. "Stand away from her now. Give her room."

The pony rested for a few minutes. She turned her head weakly. It was as though she were finding her way back from a dream. Ginny could see blood on the pony's legs. It was just above her hooves and behind her knees. She took a deep breath but kept still.

Suddenly the pony pushed herself to her feet. She wobbled a little but stood on all four legs. She took one step forward. Then another. The pony put her head down. She shook herself like a dog. Then she started to graze.

Ginny burst into tears again. "I never saw anything so stupid!" she said. "Five minutes ago we thought she was dead. Now she's eating like nothing happened at all!"

Mr. Anderson shook his head. "Amazing," he said. "I'm beginning to think that caring for a pony is not quite as simple as one might imagine."

"Bring her along up to the house, Ginny," said Mrs. Anderson. "She's got some pretty bad rope burns on her legs. We'll have to take care of them. I have some healing ointment that should be just right."

Ginny sighed. Her knees were still shaking from her fear and the relief of knowing her pony was going to be all right. "We've got an awful lot to learn, Mokey," she said. "I hope you can live through it."

Since Mokey was very stiff and sore, they slowly made their way back up the hill.

Chapter Five

Mokey's legs were painfully swollen the next day. Both Ginny and her mother looked closely at the rope burns in the brighter light of morning. They agreed that they did not look any worse than they had the night before.

They put more ointment on every sore place they could find. Then Ginny led the pony slowly down to the long grass near the oak tree. She let her graze in the sun.

Ginny glanced at her watch. It was almost eleven o'clock. She remembered with horror that she was supposed to meet Pam for a ride. Mokey would not be hurried back up the hill to the stall in the garage. It hurt her too much to walk fast. She didn't want to be shut up, anyway. Ginny finally eased her into her stall. She rushed to the telephone.

Pam had left the house by then, of course. Ginny groaned under her breath. "It is very important that Pam gets this message," Ginny said. "I was supposed to ride with her today, but . . ." She stopped. She was too embarrassed to admit what had happened. "Could you just tell her, please, that my pony is a little lame this morning? I'll call her again sometime soon."

The polite voice on the other end of the phone said that the message would be sent to the stables right away. Ginny hung up. She felt both guilty and relieved. Maybe by the time she saw Pam again, Mokey would be all better. No one outside the family would ever have to know how dumb she had been to let her own pony get hurt.

It was a few days before Mokey could walk easily again. "The only reason she's not lame,"

Ginny told her mother, "is that all her legs hurt so much. She doesn't know where to limp the most." Ginny led her pony at a slow walk for a half hour twice a day. Slowly the swelling went away and the burns began to heal.

Ginny saw Pam in town one morning. They both smiled politely at each other. They said "hello." But neither girl said anything more. Ginny's mother gave her daughter a quick look. "Wasn't that the Jennings girl?" she asked. "I didn't know you knew her."

"I don't. Not really, I mean," said Ginny. She didn't try to explain about the ride that had been forgotten in the worry over Mokey. *It all sounded too stupid,* she thought angrily. The whole thing had been dumb. She simply didn't want to talk about it.

Mokey was much better, anyway. That was all that really mattered. The last of her shabby winter coat had finally shed out. It left her smooth and shining, though to Ginny's worried eye she still looked thin. Mokey's black tail was now free of mats and burrs. It grew long and full. Her white mane and black fore-lock at last gave up their tangles to Ginny's careful brushing.

The day after the accident with the rope, Ginny's father got what looked to Ginny like a mountain of posts and rails. He dug many deep holes until a wide-fenced paddock went around the big oak. When the last rail had been slid into place, Ginny led Mokey through the gate. She turned her loose with a wave.

"My back is never going to be the same again," said Mr. Anderson cheerfully. "But it looks very nice. And Mokey will be safe. She's looking great, Ginny. You're doing a wonder-ful job with her."

The whole family leaned on the top rail. They watched proudly as the pony cantered across the paddock. She was very happy with her freedom. She stopped to lie down and roll. And then she began to graze.

* * *

It was hot that afternoon. Instead of walking Mokey up and down the driveway as she had been doing, Ginny led her along the path through the woods. It was much cooler there. Their feet barely made a sound on the deep, loamy path. It was a sudden surprise when a tall chestnut pony spun around a bend in the path. He and his rider came to a short, hard stop in front of them.

The chestnut pony half reared. He tried to

spin around. The girl on his back dropped her hands. She held him steady without seeming to move in the saddle. "Stop it, you nitwit pony," his rider said calmly. "Ginny, hi! What happened? Did you have a fall?"

Ginny shook her head. "Gosh, I'm sorry we surprised your pony like this," she finally said. "I'm fine. It's good to see you again."

Pam dismounted. She patted her dancing pony on his sweaty neck. Then she led him

toward Ginny and Mokey. "If you and Mokey are both fine, how come you aren't riding?" There was real concern in Pam's voice. Suddenly Ginny was telling her the whole story.

"So, you see," she finished, "I felt like a total fool about the whole thing. And I'm not sure whether I should ride Mokey or not. Those darned burns still look pretty bad."

"You know what you could do if you'd like," said Pam. "You could bring her over to our place and ask Michael. He's been with horses so long. He'd know what to do."

"That would be wonderful. If you don't think he'd mind," said Ginny gratefully. Leading their ponies, the two girls went through a white gate, across a wide field, and into the stable yard.

Red flowers bloomed in white wooden tubs on the low wall around the yard. The lovely shining heads of several horses looked over the low doors. They took a calm interest in the new arrivals. At the sound of hooves on the smoothly raked gravel yard, a man came out the open stable doors. He was of medium height. He had a touch of gray in his hair and the brightest blue eyes Ginny had ever seen.

"Hi, Michael. It's okay. I didn't fall off," said Pam quickly. "I found a friend in the woods. She needs some advice. Ginny, this is Michael."

"Hello." Ginny and Michael smiled at each other. Then Michael turned to take the chestnut pony's reins. "He's hot, Miss Pam," Michael scolded. "I'll sponge him off and cool him out first."

"He fusses all the time when he's by himself," said Pam. "He's not much fun to ride alone."

The chestnut pony danced his way across the stable yard. Michael walked quietly at his head. Ginny noticed that Michael limped a bit.

"Michael was a steeplechase jockey in England for years," Pam told Ginny. They sat on the low wall to wait. "He had a bad fall, so he can't be a jockey anymore. But he's still a great rider. And he's wonderful with horses." The two girls sat swinging their legs on the warm stones. Mokey nibbled without much interest on the leaf of a flower. Then she stood quietly. The ends of the reins were in Ginny's hand.

It didn't seem long before Michael came back. "Now, then," he said briskly. "What seems to be the problem?"

He asked polite questions and left time for Ginny's answers. But Ginny could tell that he had seen everything in his first sweeping look at her pony. He bent over and picked up Mokey's front leg. He let the hoof down gently. He patted the pony. Then he said to Ginny, "Bring her along inside. We'll fix her up soon."

It was cool and quiet in the wide aisle between the two rows of stalls. Mokey stood patiently. She looked around with interest. The brass rings beside the stalls were glowing softly with polish. A darkly shining leather halter with a brass nameplate hung beside each stall door. Dark wood paneling and a black iron grille went around each large stall. Behind it, Ginny could just see the heads of the gleaming horses. She could hear them moving about quietly in their deep, clean beds of straw.

Michael came up to Mokey with a small clipping machine. It was hardly bigger than his hand. He let Mokey sniff at it. Then he plugged it in and turned it on. It made almost no sound. Unsure, Mokey blew at it once or twice. Then she relaxed and paid no attention. Michael spoke quietly to the pony. He began to move the clipping machine gently near her muzzle.

"We'll just let her get used to it for a bit," he said. "I doubt this pony has ever seen a clipping machine before. Have you had her long, Miss Ginny?"

Ginny told him about Mokey. She watched in wonder as Michael clipped the long hairs from Mokey's muzzle. He trimmed the insides and edges of her ears. He started to clip away at her mane, just behind her ears.

"You're not going to cut it all off!" gasped Ginny.

"No, silly," laughed Pam. "Only that little bit where the bridle goes behind her ears. It keeps the mane much neater. Michael does it to all our horses."

Michael patted Mokey. "Nice little mare," he said. "Has a lot of sense. Now, let's get to these fetlocks of yours." He ran the clipping machine over the round joints above Mokey's hooves. The shaggy hair fell away. He clipped around the burns below the fetlocks. He went to get a bucket of warm water. He gently sponged the sore places. When the hair had dried, he clipped above the hooves again. Finally he nodded. He stood up and turned off the clipping machine.

"Getting all that hair away from those burns will help them heal more quickly," he said to Ginny. "I'll give you a jar of a different kind of ointment. Use it lightly. Just a very little bit, once a day." He put the clippers away and went to get the ointment.

When he came back, he gave Ginny a jar. He also gave her a small white plastic container. "Give her this powder in her feed tonight," he said. "I don't think this pony's been wormed for some time. This medicine should help her pick up. She'll look better very soon."

"She looks so much nicer already after what you've done," said Ginny. "Thank you so much. I had no idea how much difference clipping those little bits could make."

"Don't rush off just yet," said Michael. "Two more things. You can ride her now. Just go easy for another day or two. And this pony needs shoeing. Badly. Do you see how long her toes have grown? And how they are chipping around the edges?"

"Gosh," said Ginny. She kneeled to look at the chips that Michael showed her. "I hadn't thought about that. Mr. Dobbs didn't say anything about it. Do you suppose she's ever had shoes on in her life? Why don't those chipped places turn into cracks?"

"They will if she isn't shod," said Michael. "The blacksmith is coming here tomorrow morning. He's going to reset a shoe on Mr. Jennings's black colt. Would you like to bring your pony over and let him see to her if he has the time?"

Ginny felt her face getting red. "I feel I'm being an awful pest," she said finally. "You've been so nice. You've taken so much time this afternoon. I don't want to get in your way."

"Don't be silly," Pam said quickly. "Michael never minds when someone really wants to learn about horses. Do you, Michael?"

"But there seems to be so much I don't know," said Ginny. She looked at her pony sadly.

"You will never feel you know enough," Michael agreed cheerfully. "No matter how many years you spend with horses, there will always be something new to learn. That's what makes them so interesting. Off you go now, you two. I have other work to get done. You will have your pony here for the blacksmith in the morning, Miss Ginny?"

Ginny smiled gratefully. "We'll be here," she promised.

Chapter Six

Mokey did not like the pink powdered medicine in her grain that evening. She rattled the feed tub with her muzzle. She blew through her nostrils in annoyance. She didn't like the strange taste. She tried to eat the oats without eating any of the powder. But when Ginny went to say good night to her, Mokey had eaten all the grain and the medicine.

Mokey didn't like the sight of the smoke from the blacksmith's fire the next morning either. She slid to a stop. She threw her head in the air when she saw the blacksmith's truck. The hot coals were in a portable metal stand beside it. Ginny nearly went off over

Mokey's shoulder. She managed to save herself by grabbing wildly at Mokey's shaggy mane.

The blacksmith made disapproving noises when he looked at Mokey's hooves. After a few wary snorts, the pony stood quietly. The blacksmith trimmed each hoof. He used a curved knife with a thin blade and a heavy file.

"Been some time since this pony's been seen to," the blacksmith said finally. He stood up. He frowned at Ginny. "Plain light shoe on this one. Wouldn't you say, Michael?"

Michael had been putting the black colt back in his stall. He came over and nodded good morning to Ginny. Then he spoke quietly with the blacksmith.

Ginny had not said a word during all this time. She rubbed Mokey's ears. Ginny was trying to hear what the two men were saying. She was aware that her shirttail had pulled out of the waist of her blue jeans when she had nearly fallen off Mokey.

Ginny was thinking how funny her spotted pony must look. She had unmatched eyes and mane and tail. And she was outside this perfect stable full of blooded and beautiful horses. Ginny began to feel more and more out of place. She stood beside her pony. The two smart, skilled men talked about each hoof with deep thought.

"She's only a plain pony," Ginny wanted to say. "She isn't a show pony. She isn't a racehorse. She's just Mokey." But she didn't say it. She just watched in silence. The blacksmith picked up one hoof. He held a shoe on it and shook his head. Then he went back to his truck for another shoe.

"Toes in a little on the right foreleg," said the blacksmith. "The shoe will soon mend that."

Almost two hours later, he set the last nail in the last shoe. He stepped back from the pony. He waved his hand. "Jog her out," he told Ginny.

Ginny looked helplessly at Michael. "I
don't know what that means," she whispered.

Michael smiled. He took Mokey's reins.
"He wants to see her led at a trot. Then he can
make sure she is moving evenly and straight,"
he said. "I'll take the pony." He clucked to

Mokey. She had fallen half asleep. He turned her and led her away at a trot.

"I don't believe it," Ginny said out loud. "I simply don't believe it." For the first time that morning, the blacksmith grinned at her.

"Proper shoeing makes a bit of difference," he said.

Ginny just stared. Mokey began to trot out. Her stride seemed to get longer with each step. Michael brought her back to a walk. He turned her. Then he let her go into a trot again. Mokey arched her neck. She gave a happy swish of her tail. She seemed to float over the ground.

"That pony's not a bad mover," said the blacksmith. "Given a chance, that is. Don't forget, young lady. A pony's hooves grow all the time. They're just like your fingernails. Only the poor pony has to stand on those hooves. They can get pretty sore when they aren't tended to. They grow uneven. They chip and crack. They change the whole angle of the leg when she moves. Now she's comfortable. The angle of the hoof is right. It doesn't hurt anymore when she strides out. Give her a few more months of proper shoeing. You'll see even more of a difference. Mind, this has to be done every five or six weeks."

Ginny gave the blacksmith her name and address for his billing records. She thanked him and Michael. Mokey jogged across the road on their way home. Her hoofbeats made a new and musical sound.

Two weeks later, Mokey's legs were fully healed. Ginny called Pam to ask if they could ride together the next morning. "I'm sorry. I can't tomorrow," she said. "Our new outside course is ready. They just finished putting in the stone wall yesterday. Michael says that if I don't school Firefly over some new fences pretty soon, he's going to forget how to jump." Pam laughed. "Of course that's not true. But it has been a long time. I'm going to school him tomorrow."

"Can I come and watch?" asked Ginny eagerly.

"Sure! See you tomorrow."

Ginny rode Mokey to the schooling field the next morning. Pam was warming up her pony. She waved briefly. Then she went back to her work. Ginny slid off Mokey's back. She let the pony graze at the end of the reins. Ginny watched Firefly and his intent rider.

Michael arrived and Pam stopped her pony. Ginny leaned against Mokey's shoulder and listened. Michael gave instructions and Pam nodded. The look on her face was serious and thoughtful. "Easy on this. It's your first time over a new course," Michael finished.

Pam made a wide circle. She broke the pony smoothly into a canter. Then she took him into a little bit faster but steady hand gallop. Firefly pricked his ears. He settled into an evenly paced stride. He glided over the first jump. A rail fence. A white gate. A stone wall with a heavy log on its top. Every jump was met with a prick of ears and strict attention. Pam seemed barely to move in the saddle. She finished the course and drew smoothly to a walk. Her face was flushed with pleasure.

"Very nice," said Michael. "Not perfect, mind. You must make a wider turn after the post-and-rail fence. That will give your pony a better chance to get straight at the gate jump. You like to cut your corners, Miss Pam. Take your time. Think your turns before you make them."

Pam tried the turn between the two jumps three more times. She walked her pony to rest him. Then she jumped twice more before Michael finally nodded his approval.

"Fine," he said. "A good start. We'll try again on Thursday."

Pam took off her hard black helmet. She waved it in front of her hot face. "Why don't you take Mokey around once, Ginny?" she said. "It's a lovely course."

"Oh, gosh, no," said Ginny quickly. "Mokey is fun to ride, but she's not much of a jumper. She gets up close to a jump before she'll even try to take off. Then she kind of hops over it. I've tried her at home in the paddock and over fallen logs in the woods. I don't think she likes jumping at all."

"You'd better keep that pony walking, Miss Pam," said Michael. "He's hot. And as for your pony, Miss Ginny, I think your problem is that bit you've got on her."

"Oh." Ginny looked at the metal bit in Mokey's mouth. "I never paid much attention to it. This is the bridle that came with her. So I thought it was okay."

"This is a curb bit," said Michael. "It's a very harsh bit. I think Mokey is afraid of it. When a pony jumps, it must stretch out its head and neck in the air. It does this just as it takes off and during the flight over the fence. Sometimes the rider doesn't give the pony enough rein. Or the pony is afraid of the bit. Then it will put in a short stride in front of the fence. It will jump the way you said Mokey jumps. It might be interesting to try her in a snaffle."

"What a wonderful idea," said Pam. She was listening as she walked her pony in a circle around them. "Do we still have that pony snaffle that we used on Firefly when he was younger?"

"I'm sure we do," said Michael. "I'll just have a look."

In a few minutes he was back. He had a bridle in his hand. Ginny was filled with excitement. She had taken Mokey's old bridle off. The pony had wandered into the center of the field.

"You shouldn't have done that," said Pam with concern. "She'll run away!"

"Oh, no," said Ginny. "She'll come when I call her. She always does." She raised her voice. She called to her pony. Mokey swung away from the grass she was eating. She came trotting over to Ginny.

"Fantastic," muttered Pam. She gave her sweating pony a light slap on the neck. "Did you see that, you nitwit? Next time you toss me off, remember this. Don't go running off the way you do."

Firefly walked on. He wasn't worried. Michael fitted the bridle carefully to Mokey's head. He made sure the bit rested with ease in her mouth. "This snaffle is gentle," he told Ginny. "Work her around a few minutes to get her used to it. Then jump her over the low part of the rail fence. Wait. Just a moment. Do you have a helmet?"

Ginny shook her head. Pam rode over. She gave her helmet to Ginny. "This should fit well enough!" she said. Ginny pushed it down on her head. The helmet was hard and covered in velvet.

"It feels funny," she said.

"You'll get used to it very quickly," said Pam.

"You must never jump without a helmet," said Michael firmly. "It will protect your head in case you have a fall. All set? Then give it a try."

Ginny flung herself on Mokey's back. She urged Mokey into a trot. The pony mouthed the light snaffle bit. She tossed her head and swung into a strong canter.

"Good!" called Michael. "Let her move on, Miss Ginny!" Ginny turned the pony toward the low fence.

Mokey made her stride shorter. She slowed as she reached the fence. She bounced over it clumsily.

"Did you see that?" Ginny said. "She's hopeless."

"Nonsense," said Michael. "You must make her understand that she is to gallop and jump right in stride. When she does, you will be with her. She needs to trust herself and trust

you not to hurt her mouth. Then she'll surprise you with what she can do."

"Okay," said Ginny. She was unsure. She grabbed hold of the mane. She gave her pony a halfhearted kick. They crept over the rail fence for the second time.

"No," said Michael. "Try again."

Everything then became a blur to Ginny. The hot, sunny field. The feeling of the unsure pony under her. The hateful rail fence.

Michael's stern voice. "No. No, no. That isn't good enough. Try it again."

Finally Ginny was on the verge of tears. She didn't know what else to do. She reached back. She gave Mokey a stinging slap with her hand. Shocked, the pony galloped toward the fence. She pricked her ears. Then she swept over it with a foot to spare.

"Wow!" said Ginny. "So that's what you meant!"

"Fantastic!" cried Pam.

"Again," said Michael. This time he sounded pleased.

It was a wonderful morning. Ginny and Mokey jumped fence after fence. They grew more confident. Michael called out crisp instructions. Pam shrieked with delight at each jump.

When Ginny finally pulled up, she was speechless with happiness. Michael was nodding with quiet approval.

"You're on your way now," said Michael to Ginny. "But no more jumping until you get a helmet of your own. There are three rules of jumping. You must always keep them in mind. Give your horse a chance. Never jump without a helmet. Never jump alone."

He gave Mokey a pat. "You two girls get off those ponies now," he said. "They've done enough for one day."

Pam told Ginny that the snaffle bridle could be Mokey's for the rest of the summer.

The old pony bridle was cleaned. Then it was put away in a dim corner of the garage.

In the days that followed, the two girls rode together through the countryside. They found low walls and fences and fallen logs to jump. Some days Pam was busy with other plans. Then Ginny rode alone. She was happy to be with her pony. She liked the soft welcome stillness of the woods and open fields.

Sometimes Michael joined the two girls. He exercised one of the horses in his care. Pam's mother and father were away for the summer. They left a housekeeper in charge at home. "My father says they're off on a business trip," Pam told Ginny. "But I'll bet he manages to see a horse or two in Ireland. He doesn't like his black colt much. He might just send a new one home to replace him."

Ginny just smiled in silence. She thought briefly of her own desperate search for just one good pony in the mud and cold at the Sweetbriar Pony Farm.

Michael gave his praise. Pam gave her excited support. But Ginny could not believe that she and Mokey could jump anything but low fences.

Then, one early misty morning, the girls were chased by what they quickly decided was an angry bull. They flew on their ponies across the pasture. But the gate leading out of the field was closed and locked.

"It's okay," Pam called back, "I'm sure we can jump it." But the ground in front of the gate was rough and stony. Firefly wouldn't jump. He ducked to one side.

"Go on with Mokey!" cried Pam.

Ginny, with sudden will, gave the pony a touch of her heel. She could feel Mokey galloping. But time stood still. The bars of the green gate stood dark and clean against the cloudy sky. Then the gate was behind them. They were galloping across the next field. Mokey was bucking with delight. Ginny was laughing and gasping for breath, hanging on to the mane.

Dizzy with pride, Ginny finally pulled up. She turned in time to see Firefly land over the gate. He came cantering over to Mokey. "That was a big one," said Pam with contentment.

It had started to rain. They rode quietly across the field and into the dripping woods. "I wonder," said Ginny, "if I will ever again, in my whole life, jump anything that looks as big as that great green gate did this morning." She rested one hand on Mokey's warm, wet shoulder. "That was only a cow back there in that field, you know. It wasn't a bull. I think we knew it all the time."

"Of course," agreed Pam.

Proud and contented, the girls and their ponies made their way home.

Chapter Seven

It was going to be another scorcher of a day. Ginny woke up. She frowned at the sun. It was rising in a great orange ball. It meant there was still another day of the heat wave.

Ginny slid out of bed and tugged on her clothes. Then she stuffed her feet into a pair of sneakers. She ran a brush through her long hair. If she was going to ride at all today, it was clear that she'd better ride early. The morning air would still be cool.

She tied her hair back with a rubber band. She stuffed a few lumps of sugar into her blue jeans pocket. She tiptoed through the kitchen and took the bridle from the hook in the garage. Then she started down the hill to Mokey's paddock.

It had been so hot during these last few days. The horseflies had gotten really bad. Mokey had been spending the days in the cool stall in the garage. She spent the nights out in the paddock. She had eaten every blade of grass in the paddock. She ate right down to the bare earth. Ginny gave her an armful of hay and a tub of fresh water every evening. The pony seemed to enjoy the new setup.

"Mokey!" Ginny called softly. But there was no whinny to answer. Ginny stopped at the paddock gate. She called again. It took her several baffled moments. Then she realized that there was no pony anywhere in the pad-dock. Mokey was gone.

Once she was over her first shock, Ginny saw the rails down in one panel of the fence. She saw the faint trace of a track. It went through the dew-soaked orchard grass outside the paddock. Then it led up toward the driveway.

After the first moment of alarm, Ginny smiled to herself. The pony had probably gone over to Pam's stable, looking for company. Ginny went to get her bicycle out of the garage. She was annoyed to find that the front tire was almost flat. The bike hadn't been used since the day Mokey came.

She found the bicycle pump. She fixed the tire. Then she set off down the driveway. It was a strange feeling to be riding a bike again after so long. For the millionth time, Ginny decided that it couldn't take the place of a pony.

Ginny hummed softly under her breath. She rode along the road. She watched for signs of hoofprints. She looked on both sides for her wandering pony. But there were no signs of Mokey anywhere.

The Jennings horses were being fed. Ginny could hear the rumble of the feed cart in the aisle of the stable. She propped her bike against the wall. She poked her head through the door. Michael was away on his vacation. A strange young man was caring for the horses while he was away.

"Morning," said Ginny. "I've lost my pony. I thought she might have come here."

"Sorry, miss. I haven't seen her." The young man came to the door. He looked out over the fields. "But if she does show up, I'll be glad to put her in the extra stall and give you a call."

"That would be wonderful. Thanks." Ginny gave him her name and phone number. He wrote them down carefully on the notepad by the stable telephone.

Ginny sat on her bike for a few minutes. She was trying to make up her mind about what to do next. Pam was away. Her parents had come home and insisted she go with them for a few days in the mountains. So she couldn't help.

Ginny was starting to worry. Just a little.

She had been so sure Mokey would have come to the Jennings stable to visit Firefly. It was a surprising letdown not to have found her here.

Ginny decided to ride home on the bridle path through the woods. Just in case Mokey had chosen that way to come. There were roots and stones in the path. She had never noticed them while riding Mokey. They made bike riding hard.

She came out on the road again. She was cross and out of breath. She hadn't seen so much as a hoofprint anywhere. Not even in the soft ground near the stream. She rode home and flung the bike into the garage. Then she stormed into the kitchen. Her mother and father were having breakfast.

"That dumb pony has run away," she told them. "Vanished. In fact, she must have flown. I can't even find a hoofprint." Suddenly, to her horror, she felt tears burning her eyes. "I don't even know where to look for her!"

"Breakfast," Mrs. Anderson said firmly. "At least a glass of milk. You can't go looking for ponies on an empty stomach. And then I think we should call the police."

"The police?" said Ginny. She was startled out of the coming tears. "What for?"

"Maybe someone has seen her," said Mr. Anderson. "If you found a strange pony wandering about in your vegetable garden, wouldn't you notify the police? That is very likely where she'll be found. And does that pony ever stop eating?"

Ginny had to laugh. "That's probably why she got out," she admitted. "I think she pushed the fence rails down to get at the grass outside the paddock. There isn't any left at all inside the fence."

The police were polite and wanted to help. But they had no word of a found pony. They promised to watch for her. They would report any news as soon as they got it.

The hot day grew hotter. It dragged on

without end. Mr. Anderson pulled on his hiking boots. He set out through the woods to look for Mokey. Mrs. Anderson drove around the nearby roads in the car. Ginny stayed home to answer the phone if anyone called. But there were no calls. Mrs. Anderson finally came home. She was shaking her head. Ginny went off on her bike again.

It was late afternoon. Ginny was so tired and worried. She felt almost numb. But anything was better than just sitting still and waiting for the telephone to ring.

She rode up a number of strange driveways. She knocked on many doors. Everyone was kind and concerned. But no one had seen a lost brown and white spotted pony—or any other pony—that day.

There was a long, sweeping blue gravel driveway. It led to a house that could barely be seen from the road. Ginny turned her bike. She went through the stone pillars at the entrance. She found her tired legs would not pedal her bike through the deep gravel. She stopped. Then she left her bike and walked toward the house on foot.

She came around a last sweep of the drive and stopped so quickly that she slid. Beside the house, a pretty young woman was leaning on a low white fence. It went around an apple orchard. And there, under the apple trees, was Mokey. She was eating as usual without worries.

The woman turned. She smiled at Ginny. "Hello," she said in a warm, friendly voice. "Is this your pony? We've so liked having her with us today. The gardener found her here this morning. She looked so pretty under the apple trees. We were happy to have her stay a little while."

Ginny felt half choked with a crazy mix of rage and relief. She jammed her hands deep into her pockets. She took a long, deep, shaky breath. "We've been a little worried about her," she was able to say at last. "We didn't know where she was."

The woman waved her hands helplessly. "My husband and I have just moved here from the city. We thought this visit from your pony was one of the charming things that happen in the country."

Ginny decided quickly not to say anything more. That was safer. She hurried to her pony. Mokey raised her head from the green apples she had been eating on the ground. She slobbered apple juice cheerfully down the front of Ginny's shirt. Ginny flung her arms around the pony's neck. She wept briefly and thankfully into her mane.

Of course she had not thought to bring the bridle this time. For one moment she had a flash of panic. She was thinking she might have to leave Mokey here. Now that she had found her at last, this seemed unbearable. Even for just a few minutes. But then she thought to tug her belt from her blue jeans. She looped it around Mokey's neck, just behind her ears. She led her proudly through the narrow gate.

"We would love to have her come visit us again," the young woman called to Ginny.

"Thank you. That would be very nice," Ginny managed to say. She felt a little kinder now that she had Mokey safely by her side. After all, she told herself firmly, these people had never lived outside a city before. They might really think that ponies roamed loose in orchards all the time. Ginny even found herself smiling. Mokey must have enjoyed being admired like a fine painting.

It was wonderful to have her safely home again. The police were told and thanked. Mokey was sweaty and covered with fly bites. Ginny washed her off with warm water. Ginny stopped fussing over her and shut her firmly in the stall. The pony's usual cheerful mood had turned quite sour by this time. Ginny was sure this was due to too many hours in the heat and flies. She gave the pony a full bucket of fresh cool water. Mokey drank it. Then Ginny gave Mokey her evening feed of grain and hay. This did not seem to interest her very much. Ginny left her alone.

It was over. Ginny felt as limp as a soapy sponge. Her mother and father were as tired and relieved as she was. Dinner became a happy celebration.

"Your father and I had planned to go to the movies tonight," Mrs. Anderson said after the dishes were done. "Would you like to come with us?"

Ginny shook her head wearily. "No, thanks. I'm going to take a bath and wash my hair. I'm not going to move again until morning!"

It was after ten o'clock. Ginny finished brushing her hair dry. She was ready for bed. Happy and half asleep, she was in her bathrobe and slippers. She went to say a last good-night to her pony.

She turned on the garage light and went over to the stall. She had a lump of sugar in her hand. When she leaned over the door, she caught her breath. She let it out in a gasp. Mokey was standing in the middle of the stall. Her head was stuck out straight in front of her. Her nostrils were flaring as though she had been running. Her ears were back. Her eyes were staring. Her stomach was big and swollen. Sweat dripped from her shoulders and sides. She was having trouble breathing. She was clearly in great pain.

Ginny flew to the telephone to call for help. Then she stood, for a long, painful moment. She was trying to decide whom she should call. Her mother and father couldn't be reached. Michael was away. Suddenly she remembered the vet. He had cared for their cat last summer when it had cut its paw. She couldn't remember his name. She hoped wildly that his number would be listed in her mother's book of special numbers. Vet—Dr. Nichols. With shaking fingers, she dialed the number.

To her great relief, the doctor answered the telephone. "Oh, please," Ginny gasped.

"There's something terrible the matter with my pony. My parents aren't home. I don't know what to do!"

In a quiet, calming voice the doctor asked a few questions. He got Ginny's name and address. Then he said, "Don't move the pony. Take away any feed or water from the stall. Then let her alone. I'll be there in fifteen minutes."

Ginny hung up. She tore back to the stall. Mokey always finished her oats. Ginny was sure the feed tub would be empty. She was shocked to find it was not. She unclipped the hooks and set the feed tub outside the stall. She checked the water bucket. It was empty. Then she shut the stall door.

She glanced at her watch. She was frantic for something else to do. She realized suddenly that she was still in her bathrobe and slippers. She rushed upstairs. She got dressed. Then she rushed down again. She turned on all the outside lights so that the vet could find the house more easily.

A few minutes later, she saw headlights coming down the drive. Without a wasted moment, the doctor lifted his black bag from the front seat of the car. He followed Ginny to the pony's stall.

One quick glance at the sick pony was all he needed. "What did she get into?" he asked sharply. A small bottle and a syringe were already in his hand. "Grain? Bran? Corn?"

Ginny stared at him blankly. "Oh!" she cried suddenly. She had a flash of understanding. "Apples! It must be the apples! She's been eating apples in an orchard all day long!"

"Put her halter on," Dr. Nichols said briefly. Ginny snatched the halter from its hook. Then she slipped it gently over the pony's head. The syringe was filled by now. The needle bit into the pony's neck. Mokey never moved. A second shot from another vial came after the first.

The doctor went on working over the gasping pony. The silence was broken only when he spoke to Mokey in a low, calming

voice. Finally he folded his stethoscope. He
took a deep breath. Then he left the stall.
"Now we wait," he said. "And this is the hard-

est part of all. Twenty minutes." He checked the time on his watch.

"You aren't going to leave?" asked Ginny. Her voice was shaky.

"Of course not." He sat on a bale of hay. He turned so that he could watch the still pony. "Now tell me what happened," he said.

Ginny told the story of the long and frantic day. The doctor shook his head. "Apples," he said, "can be very bad. They go sour when they get into the stomach. But too much grain can be just as dangerous. Or even too much grass, if the pony isn't used to it. Horses and ponies can kill themselves by eating too much. Most other animals have more sense. I like horses. I've owned and cared for them all my life. But they really seem to go out of their way to get themselves into trouble."

Ginny nodded. "But I've eaten too many apples," she said. "I've gotten a stomachache sometimes. Once they made me sick. But Mokey looks"—she stopped and caught her breath— "she looks as though she might even die."

The doctor did not disagree with her. Ginny had hoped he would. "She has a pretty bad case of colic," he said finally. "Horses and ponies can't vomit like dogs or cats or people. That's why your pony is in so much trouble. All those apples. And probably a bucket of water on top of them—" Ginny nodded sadly. "Her stomach is so swollen. We can only hope it doesn't burst before the medicine has time to work."

"If it bursts, she'll die," Ginny said flatly.

"That's right. I really am sorry to have to tell you all this. I want you to be prepared. Just in case. It's a good thing you called me as quickly as you did."

He checked his watch and got up. Then he gave Mokey two more shots and another dose of medicine. The sweet, sharp smell filled the garage. Ginny peeked nervously at the pony in the stall. "She's not sweating so much," she said hopefully.

"That's only because I've given her something to relieve the pain," said the doctor. "This kind of thing is agony. At least she's not hurting so much now."

He stood for a moment. He watched with concern. The pony tried hard to breathe. "I wish there were a large animal hospital nearby. Or a veterinary school with an operating room for horses. Then we might be able to get her there and operate in time. But the nearest one is several hundred miles from here. In the shape she's in, the trip alone would probably kill her."

They waited in silence. A moth fluttered around the lightbulb in the ceiling. Outside the garage door the crickets and locusts were making cheerful night noises. But inside there was a strange quiet. Finally Ginny realized that she was missing the sound of Mokey moving around in her stall. Crunching her hay. Rattling her feed tub hopefully every once in a while.

The doctor rose to his feet. He checked the pony again with his stethoscope. For the first time that night, he smiled. More shots. More medicine. Then he nodded to Ginny. "Progress," he reported. "I really think she's going to make it after all."

The hours went by in a gray haze. Ginny's mother and father came back from the movies. They were told what had happened. They made coffee. They asked brief, worried questions about the sick pony.

Dawn came. The sun rose. At seven o'clock, Dr. Nichols checked the pony again. By this time, Mokey was poking her muzzle cheerfully into every corner of her stall. She was looking for a stray wisp of hay or one tiny spilled grain of oats to eat. Her stomach was back to normal size. There was a light gray film of dried sweat on her sides and shoulders. Other than that, there was not a sign that anything had been the matter with her at all.

"I'll just bet," said Ginny wearily, "that she'd eat all those apples again, right now."

"She certainly would," agreed the doctor. "A lot of caring for horses and ponies is protecting them from their own foolishness." He snapped the clasp shut on his black bag. "You can give her two swallows of warmed water every hour. But nothing to eat. I'll be back this evening after office hours to check her again." He rumpled Mokey's black forelock. Ginny thought he looked almost as tired, and just as glad, as she felt herself.

"To bed with you, young lady," her mother said firmly to Ginny. The doctor drove away. "I can give that pony of yours two swallows of water. Yes, I know. Warmed once every hour."

Still saying that she wanted to take care of Mokey herself, Ginny stumbled up the stairs. She barely managed to kick her sneakers off. Then she threw herself on her bed and fell asleep.

Chapter Eight

Ginny stood by the gate to the white-fenced show ring. Cheery marching music came from the loudspeakers. Red and white flags snapped in the brisk early-morning breeze. They marked the outside course. Ponies of all sizes and shapes whirled in circling patterns. They were all across the vivid green of the polo field where the show was being held.

The music stopped. The speaker's low, clear voice sounded across the field. It was calling the first class of the day.

"Model ponies, large group. Bring your ponies to the ring, please."

Ginny backed away. The wide gate swung

open. A crowd of gleaming ponies rushed into the ring. All of them were without saddles. They were led by their riders on foot. This class was to be judged only on the ponies' looks. Pam was in the ring with her coppery Firefly. As usual, he was dancing at the end of his reins. There were bays and blacks and browns and grays. But no spots, Ginny saw. All the ponies had their manes done up in small braids. The tops of their tails were braided as well.

Ginny shook with excitement. Pam had finally talked her into entering Mokey in this show. The pony was waiting in Pam's trailer in the shade of the huge old oaks on the edge of the polo field. Michael had spent the past week teaching Ginny how to shorten and thin out the pony's mane. Then he taught her how to do it up in braids.

Ginny found that it took a lot of practice. The first five or six times she'd tried it, the mane wasn't short enough. The braids were limp and lumpy. Finally, though, even Michael had to nod his approval.

The braiding of the tail had been a different matter. Thinking about it, Ginny made a face. She knew how it was done. She pulled the first few strands at the top of the tail tightly. It looked nice when it was finished. But the moment Mokey switched her tail at a fly, the whole thing started to come apart. Ginny tried so many times. Even Mokey became impatient. Michael finally came to the rescue. He told her to let it be. He said that he would do it for her the morning of the show.

Now Mokey was waiting for her first class. Her mane was done up. Her smartly braided tail (thanks to Michael) was snugly wrapped in a protective bandage. Ginny stood by the ring. She watched Pam's first class.

The two judges were walking slowly around each pony. They stood back to get an overall picture. Then they went on to the next and moved the ponies into two lines.

Firefly was standing with his weight properly balanced on all four legs. His red-gold coat was shimmering in the sunlight. His small ears pricked toward Pam.

The winners were announced. A pewter-gray pony left the ring. He had a snow-white mane and tail. The blue ribbon hung from his bridle. A rather unkind look of success was on his owner's face. Pam held Firefly back. They let the gray go through the gate. Then she followed him out. She handed Firefly's reins, and the second-place red ribbon, to Michael.

"Very nice, Miss Pam," said Michael. He threw a wide light wool blanket over the chestnut pony. "We'll just get this cooler on you, young fellow. The breeze is still a bit fresh this time of day." He was whistling cheerfully. He led the pony back toward the trailer. Pam came over to join Ginny at the ring fence.

"That gray is a lovely pony," Pam said. She was excited. "He's an English Anglo-Arab— half Thoroughbred and half Arabian. This is the first time I've seen him. He's only been in this country about six weeks."

Pam glanced at her watch. "Your first class is coming up in half an hour. You'd better get Mokey."

Ginny stomped along beside Pam. They were on the way over to the trailer. Ginny's new riding boots felt stiff and heavy. Her breeches felt strange. She was sure she was slowly choking in her long-sleeved shirt. It had a tight collar and tie.

They reached the trailer. Ginny struggled into her new blue riding coat. She crammed her black helmet on top of her head. She looked at Mokey gloomily. "You," she whispered crossly to Mokey. "You are pretending to be something you aren't. I have never seen so many great ponies in one place in my entire life. I can't imagine what we are doing here." Mokey helped herself to another mouthful of hay. It was from the rope net tied high in front of her. She sneezed. Then she went on eating.

Michael put Firefly into the stall next to the trailer. He backed Mokey carefully down the ramp. He slipped her bridle on. Ginny protested. "Honestly, Michael, don't bother. I can do that myself!" He put the saddle onto Mokey's back.

"She looks sort of strange," said Ginny. She was unsure.

Pam laughed. "You're just not used to seeing her all braided up and with a saddle on her," she said. "But you can't very well ride her bareback today! Just be glad we were able to borrow one that fit her."

Michael waved to Ginny. "Give you a leg up for luck," he said. He swung Ginny up into the saddle. Ginny grabbed for her stirrups. She decided they were too long. She made them shorter. Then she changed her mind. She let them down again. She had practiced with Mokey for several days. They had used Pam's saddle. But it still felt strange. She had ridden the pony bareback for so long.

Mokey stood patiently. Ginny fiddled about with her stirrups and reins. Michael took off the tail bandage. He checked the tightness of the girth. He went over the pony one more time with a soft cloth.

"Bring your ponies to the ring gate," the loudspeaker called. "For Class Eleven, Pony Working Hunters, over the outside course."

"Now, remember," said Pam. She was walking beside Mokey. "The looks of the ponies don't count in this class. They are judged only on their manners. And on how they perform over the outside course. And on the way they move and jump."

"Okay," said Ginny. Then, faintly, "I think I'm going to be sick to my stomach."

"No, you're not," said Pam firmly. "Take deep breaths. We'll get your number listed. We'll find out how soon your turn is. Then you'd better get busy warming up."

"Okay," whispered Ginny. Pam checked in at the gate. She found Mokey would be the seventh to go on the course. Then Ginny trotted Mokey far out on the polo field. She was alone on her pony. She began to feel much better once they were trotting and cantering in wide circles on the smooth grass.

She caught sight of Pam waving to her. It was much too soon. She turned Mokey back toward the ring. She didn't want to go.

"You're next," said Pam.

"Yuck," said Ginny.

Pam stepped back with an understanding grin. The wide white gate swung open. Mokey walked into the ring.

Ginny was numb with nervousness. Somehow she managed to gather her reins into a short tangle. She pushed Mokey into a canter. She circled toward the first jump. Mokey raised her head. She pricked her ears.

"Oh, gosh," cried Pam to Michael. "I never thought! I'll bet Mokey has never seen a brush fence in her life!"

Mokey never had seen such a thing.

Neither had Ginny. It was nothing more than short evergreen branches. They were packed tightly into a long white wooden stand. But it looked hairy and huge. Mokey stopped. She was unsure. Ginny sat unmoving in the saddle. She completely forgot everything she had practiced so hard, so many times, in the schooling field. The confused pony slowed to a trot.

Ginny became aware that things were not right. From some dim working corner of her mind, she remembered to give Mokey a kick to prompt her. Then she grabbed hold of the braided mane.

Mokey felt more sure that she really was supposed to jump that strange green thing in front of her. She trotted forward. She jumped the brush with a giant spring. It tossed Ginny up onto her neck. She was gasping. Then she came back with a jolt into the saddle.

Mokey landed. She cantered on. Ginny poked her feet back into the stirrups. She tipped her helmet back in the right place. She

pulled herself together before they came to the next fence. It was a very comfortable-looking stone wall. And it was of a size and type they had jumped many times before this.

Mokey jumped it well. The course swung to the left. It went between two flags. Ginny began riding her pony instead of just sitting in a helpless lump. They began to enjoy themselves. Over a gate. Neatly through an in-and-out. Then a zigzag rail fence. Two more fences. And then they finished the course over a last brush fence. It was the twin of the first. It led back into the ring. Mokey jumped this with ease. She even bobbed her head. She gave a flip of her tail as she landed. She was clearly pleased with herself and her performance. Ginny's face was glowing with delight. She pulled Mokey up and trotted from the ring.

"Wasn't she wonderful?" she gasped. She flung herself out of the saddle. She gave Mokey a hug. Pam and Michael joined in warm congratulations. The unlucky first jump was talked about only indirectly. Mokey was being sponged off and walked in the shade.

"You'll be all right from now on, Miss Ginny," Michael said kindly. "There can't ever be another first fence in your first class in your first show."

"Thank goodness for that," said Ginny.

Chapter Nine

The show went on through the morning. Pam won a big class with Firefly over the outside course. Then they won another in the ring. The beautiful gray pony was named Ashes. He did not jump very well in his hunter class. "He's young and still very new to this," said Pam. But he went very well in the walk, trot, and canter class in the ring. He and Firefly were chosen to work together for several minutes. Then the judges' decision went to Pam's pony.

It was clear that the girl on the gray pony was not at all pleased with the way things were going. When the judges weren't looking, she briefly let her pony bump up against Firefly.

There was an instant of confusion. The girl on the gray said she was sorry sweetly to Pam. Pam smiled back politely. But then she moved Firefly to the far side of the ring.

The chestnut pony was upset, Ginny saw with a sinking heart. She could see the white showing around his eyes. His ears were flicking back and forth. They always did when he was nervous. Ginny thought that Pam was probably angry. But she saw that Pam's face stayed calm and unruffled. She spoke softly to her pony. She soon had him settled down.

"What was that all about?" asked Ginny. The class was over. "Was all that fuss on purpose? Or was it an accident? It was hard to tell."

Pam's mouth set briefly into a grim line. "That Angela Longworth is a pain," she said. "Firefly hates feeling crowded. She knows it. But that new pony of hers is too nice. It doesn't need that kind of foolishness. He's good enough on his own."

*   *   *

Ginny was watching the two girls ride in a later class. She thought they made it look so easy. The two wonderful ponies moved like precision clocks. There was hardly a wasted movement by either pony or rider. "This Angela person may be a pill," Ginny said to Mokey later. "But she sure can ride." Firefly shied and played in this class. He had to be happy with a white ribbon for fourth place. The gray pony was first.

At the lunch break the two girls lay out in the shade. They had a picnic basket. Their coats were off. Their collars were open.

"You know, Ginny," Pam said at last. "I really am sorry I talked you into bringing Mokey to this show."

"What for?" gasped Ginny. She sat up in surprise.

"I don't think it was fair to start you off with such strong competition," said Pam. "It seems as though every good show pony in the country is here today. This show used to be small. It was friendly and fun. I guess I was remembering how it used to be. That's why I talked you into coming with me today."

"Never mind," said Ginny. She flopped down in the grass again. "Mokey is very special. But this is all a bit over her head. Don't worry about it, though. It's fun to be part of all this." She waved her sandwich at the polo field and the white-fenced ring.

"Anyway, we only entered her in two classes. We never did plan to make a big thing of this." She took a bite of sandwich. She mumbled around the edges. "Stop worrying. Save your energy for beating that awful Angela. You'll need it."

"But," Ginny said quietly to Mokey later. She went to put her bridle on for the next class. "It sure would be fun to win a ribbon." She sighed and patted Mokey. She felt sorry for her. Then she backed her out of the trailer.

Firefly whinnied like mad as Ginny led Mokey away. Michael was at the pony's head in a moment. He was calming him down. Ginny saddled Mokey. She trotted off to warm up. She promised herself that this time, she would keep her wits about her. She wouldn't let herself get so nervous that she forgot how to ride.

Ginny nearly managed to keep calm. Everything went well until the very last moment. She was waiting to go into the ring. She heard a shout from Michael and a shriek from Pam. She pulled Mokey out of line. She wondered with fear what she had done. "Hey, wait! Mokey still has the bandage on her tail!" cried Pam.

Ginny was upset and annoyed with herself. She felt her face growing red. Pam took hold of Mokey's bridle. She held her still. Michael swiftly took off the bandage.

"Okay now," said Pam with a giggle. "She'd have looked a little funny going around the course with that still on."

"Gosh," said Ginny. She was angry with herself. "There's so darned much to remember."

"Never you mind," Michael spoke quietly. "You just get in there with that good pony. Give her a chance to show what she can do."

"Right," Ginny said firmly. She took her reins smoothly and carefully. She rode Mokey in through the open gate.

Mokey went well, from the first green brush to the last. Ginny was very pleased. She trotted out of the ring. Michael was pleased, too. She could tell by his silent nod. He reached for Mokey's reins.

"Thanks, Michael. But I'll cool her out," said Ginny. She slid from the saddle. "Her halter is in the trailer, isn't it?"

"I wouldn't untack her just yet," said Michael. "Loosen her girth. Walk her around. You might be wanted back in the ring after a round like that."

A wave of hope swept over Ginny. "You mean we might get a ribbon?" she said weakly.

"Not for sure," warned Michael. "There are only four ribbons. But the judges will call about ten ponies back. From what I have seen of the others in this class so far, Mokey just might be one of them."

"Oh, wow," said Ginny. She walked Mokey for a few minutes. Then Michael began rubbing the pony down. Mokey wanted to eat the short, sweet grass of the polo field. She was not allowed to do so because her bit would get stained. She looked bored.

The last pony finished the course. There was a pause of several minutes. Then the loudspeaker called: "Bring the following ponies into the ring, please." Mokey's number was the fourth to be called.

"Quick, tell me what to do now," Ginny said in a panic.

"Just get on. Ride her in," said Pam. "The ringmaster will tell you what to do."

They were asked to line up in single file. They were to be in the order their numbers had been called. The judges held a short meeting. They checked the numbers on their cards. Then the ringmaster in his scarlet coat came over to Ginny. He touched his top hat. The girl on the bay was in line in front of Ginny. He asked that they change places.

This moved Mokey up to third place in line. Ginny felt she could not take one more moment of suspense. She managed to keep Mokey standing well. She tried to look like she knew what to do.

Finally one of the judges waved his card. The first pony trotted across the ring. A chestnut followed. Then Ginny on Mokey. Three or four others were called. Ginny knew all of them were being trotted out for soundness. The judges were looking to see if any of the ponies were lame. A lame pony could not win a ribbon. She knew she had nothing to worry about. Mokey was perfectly sound.

Another pause. The judges spoke to the ringmaster. He went to the announcer's stand. Mokey was tired. Ginny could feel her sigh. Mokey started to droop a little.

Some riders were dismounting and holding their ponies to rest them. Ginny did the same. She saw Michael nod his approval. He was on the side of the ring. The loudspeaker crackled briefly. The show vet was being called.

He came into the ring. He spoke to the judges. Then he walked along the line of waiting ponies. He looked them over with swift, expert care. He didn't touch them. He didn't pay any more attention to one than to another.

The ponies were then asked to jog again. This time Ginny led Mokey at a trot. Most of the others were doing the same. It must have been hot. Later, Ginny found her shirt soaking wet under her coat. Her hair was under the black helmet. It was wet as though she had been in a shower. But she didn't notice now.

The vet wrote something on each of the judges' cards. He shook hands with them and left the ring. The judges signed their cards. They handed them to the ringmaster. Then they walked across to the judges' stand.

Time stood still. Ginny could hear two other riders whispering. They were wondering which pony the judges had been unsure about. The girl with the bright bay pony was now fourth in line. She was behind Mokey. She joined them. Ginny heard her laugh. The girl said, "I just know they called the vet to look at that spotted thing. You can tell it's blind in one eye. The rules say that's an unsoundness."

Ginny felt her face flushing with anger. Mokey wasn't blind, just because her eyes didn't match! She fought to look as calm and collected as she could. Wouldn't the judges know? The vet could tell, couldn't he? After all of this awful waiting, could they take Mokey's ribbon away? Just because she had one blue eye and one brown?

At last the announcer's voice came over the loudspeakers. "We have the results of Class Twelve, Pony Working Hunters."

The blue ribbon and a silver plate were won by a boy on a seal-brown pony. The red ribbon went to a blaze-faced chestnut. Then the ringmaster was tipping his hat to Ginny. He pinned the golden yellow ribbon for third place on Mokey's bridle.

Ginny never knew who was fourth. She never remembered leaving the ring. Michael's usually stern face was full of smiles. "Very nice, Miss Ginny," he said.

Pam was speechless with delight. She gave Mokey a big hug and found her voice at last. "Terrific," she said.

They led Mokey to the trailer. The yellow ribbon was fluttering on her bridle. Quiet and happy, all three helped to take the saddle and bridle off the tired pony. They put on her

halter. Ginny held her in silence. Michael sponged her off.

When he was done, he reached for the lead rope. But Ginny shook her head. "Please," she said. "Let me take her."

She put the yellow ribbon in her pocket. She led Mokey away from the crowds and the ring. They went toward the far edge of the polo field. The grass grew long under the trees there.

Ginny sat down. She leaned back against a tree trunk. Mokey cropped the grass quietly. She was at the end of the lead rope. The late-afternoon sun slanted across the field. It was throwing long shadows and blazing in the tops of the trees.

Ginny took the ribbon out of her pocket. She smoothed it on one knee. She was in a tired haze of happiness. She put her head back. She squinted through her lashes up at the patterns of leaves above her.

Suddenly Ginny sat up. She scrambled to

her feet. The yellow ribbon had meant so much just a moment before. But now it fell into the grass. Ginny didn't notice. She looked at the branches above her.

There. She had seen it again. She didn't know why she hadn't seen it before. There was a patch of red-gold leaves just over her head.

Slowly she found the ribbon. She stuffed it into her pocket. She went over to Mokey. It wasn't just the late sunlight that was setting the trees on fire. The leaves were starting to turn. Summer was almost over.

Chapter Ten

"Of course it is all quite impossible." Mr. Anderson tapped his pipe firmly in his hand. "We have no place to keep a pony in the winter. Not even if we could afford to buy her, which I very much doubt."

"I know," Ginny said helplessly. She and her father leaned on the top rail of the paddock. They watched Mokey. She was shaking the seeds out of her hay so she could eat them by themselves.

Ginny giggled suddenly. "There was a gray pony at the show last weekend. It cost eighteen thousand dollars."

Mr. Anderson turned to stare at Ginny. He

couldn't believe it. "Now, young lady, that simply can't be true."

Ginny was sure. "Everybody at the show was talking about it. It was a beautiful pony."

"I should hope so!" said Mr. Anderson. "And I guess your wonderful Mokey beat it in the hunter class?"

Ginny giggled again. "That would be something, wouldn't it! But they weren't even in the same classes."

"Probably just as well," said her father. "It wouldn't do at all to have a rented summer pony beat eighteen thousand dollars on the hoof."

"Handsome is as handsome does," said Ginny firmly.

"Quite right."

Mokey wandered over to the paddock fence. She gazed with longing at the grass. It was out of her reach. She pushed with annoyance at the rails. They blocked her way. But each rail in the entire paddock had been

125

nailed firmly into place. That was done the day after she had escaped and found the apple orchard. She could not push them down. She gave a bored sigh. Then she turned back to her hay.

Ginny and her father walked in silence to the house. They had had this talk several times before. Mokey did not belong to them. She belonged to Mr. Dobbs. And to the awful Sweetbriar Pony Farm. She had been rented only for the summer. There was nothing, absolutely nothing, Ginny could do.

She had thought wildly of so many answers through so many sleepless nights. All of them were either crazy or impossible. She'd even thought of asking Pam if her father would buy Mokey. But then she had met Mr. Jennings one day. He was tall and scary and stern. He did not look at all like the kind of person who would take in a rather strangely spotted pony with unmatching eyes. Not in his stable full of beautiful horses.

Ginny finished cleaning Mokey's stall. She dumped the wheelbarrow down by the garden.

She had the pony bedded on peat moss now. Mokey would not eat it like she had eaten her straw bedding. This was much better for her. Mr. Anderson was happy. The peat moss was good for his beloved vegetable garden.

Ginny was tired of worrying. She was tired of not being able to find an answer. She rattled the wheelbarrow angrily back to the garage. She took the bridle off the hook. At least she could still ride. This always made her feel better.

But by now, there were too many signs that summer was over. The trees were all changing colors. In the open fields, the grass was drying to a soft russet red.

Ginny spent the whole afternoon on Mokey's back. But it did not help very much. She finally turned toward home. She knew she was being silly and unfair. She knew her mother and father felt almost as bad as she did. She promised herself not to make things any more difficult or unhappy than they already were.

Ginny was feeling older and wiser. She was happy with her decision. She jogged down the driveway. Then she pulled up with a jerk. It brought the surprised pony to a sliding stop. Mr. Dobbs's battered green pickup truck was standing by the garage.

Ginny spun Mokey around. She kicked her into a gallop. Small stones scattered wildly from the pony's flying hooves. They crossed the road. Ginny pressed her pony on deeper into the woods. It was getting darker.

There was a fallen log across the path. Ginny and Pam had jumped it a few times over the summer. It was old and streaked with moss. And it was almost impossible to see in the failing evening light. Mokey was galloping too fast. She couldn't check herself when the log loomed out of the shadows. She hit it with her knees and turned over.

*   *   *

Ginny opened her eyes and blinked with surprise. It was almost dark. Blurry stars were shining in little patches. They shone through the swaying branches of the trees. Ginny was on her back in the ferns and dead leaves beside the path. Her head ached terribly.

She sat up slowly. But the woods spun and tilted around her. They made her so dizzy she had to lie down again. The crushed ferns smelled good. She closed her eyes.

She felt a warm breath down the side of her neck. It was Mokey. She was pushing at Ginny with her muzzle. "Hi, Moke." Ginny tried to sit up again. She faintly saw the reins were broken. They were trailing in uneven lengths from the pony's bit.

Ginny held on to a tree. She swayed to her feet. She grabbed at Mokey's mane to keep her balance. "I think we've got some kind of a problem," she said in an uneven voice. "I've broken the bridle that doesn't even belong to me." It seemed a great problem.

Ginny stood by her pony. She was dizzy and worrying. "The only thing to do is go home now, I guess. And tell Pam." She turned her head slowly. It hurt. Mokey's back looked a long way up.

Ginny could never remember later how she finally managed to get on Mokey's back. Or how she had picked up the broken reins and turned toward home. The pony walked slowly. Ginny sang a little to herself. But this made her head ache more. So she went back to worrying about the broken bridle again.

There were lights on everywhere when she got home. Her head was clearing slightly. She dimly saw Michael. He was in the flood-lights outside the garage. He was up on one of Mr. Jennings's big hunters. Pam was white-faced. She was trying to calm her frantic Firefly.

"We can't find her anywhere," she heard Pam say. Then Mokey whinnied a loud greeting to Firefly.

"Hi," said Ginny. She suddenly felt very foolish. "I broke your bridle."

There were cries of relief. Then suddenly people were holding Mokey and helping Ginny down. Her knees felt very strange when she walked. But Ginny insisted on leading Mokey into the lights by the garage. She wanted to make sure the pony wasn't hurt.

"I really did it this time," Ginny said to Michael. "I jumped alone. I jumped without my helmet. I don't think I will ever do it again."

"I believe that is very true," said Michael. He said nothing more. Ginny knew that he would never talk about it again. She was grateful.

Ginny felt faint and confused. She leaned against her father's arm. "Whatever happened to Mr. Dobbs?" she asked finally. "Did he give up and go away?" Then she grinned at Mokey. "If he did, it was worth it," she said.

Mrs. Anderson came up beside her. "For two cents I'd send that pony right back where she came from!" she said in a shaking voice.

"Ginny, what a stupid thing to do! Mr. Dobbs was here because your father and I asked him to come. We wanted to find out, at least, how much he might want for Mokey."

"Oh," said Ginny. She blinked up at the lights over the garage. There seemed to her to be two lights wherever there should be just one.

"There was talk of the humane society closing his place down," said Mr. Anderson. "But now that won't have to happen. A supermarket chain has bought his land. It paid a great deal of money. He is selling off his ponies as fast as he can. It is very lucky for us because he must get rid of them. He offered us Mokey for very little more than we've already paid to rent her."

He stopped for a moment. He shook his head. "He didn't seem to think she was worth very much. But then he hasn't seen what you've done with her this summer."

"You mean that Mokey is mine?" said Ginny.

"Yes."

"And she can stay here always?"

"That's right."

"In the garage?"

"No. We've decided to keep our car for another year, not to buy a new one. We'll use the money to build a small stable down near the paddock instead."

"And so I fell on my head. And almost broke Mokey's neck. For no reason at all."

She leaned her aching head against Mokey's warm shoulder. She was surprised to feel tears sliding down her cheeks.

Mrs. Anderson quietly went into the house. She called the doctor. Then she turned down Ginny's bed. Pam and Michael whispered a smiling "good night." They rode off into the dark. Silently, Ginny looked up at her father.

"It's been quite a summer," he said.

Together, they put Mokey away in her

stall. The pony rattled her feed tub in demand. Ginny thought she was making it quite clear that there had been enough excitement for one day. It was late. It was long past dinner-time. Mokey was hungry.

Chapter Eleven

Ginny was restless in bed the next afternoon. She was bored. She no longer was seeing double. But her head ached when she tried to read.

There was a light knock on her door. Pam came in. She was holding an apple in one hand. Just as she had the first time they had met early in the summer. It seemed so long ago.

"Hi!" Pam pulled up a chair. She sat down by the bed. "You look pale and awful. Just like your mother said you did. How do you feel?"

Ginny grinned. "Fine," she said. "I'm really glad you came. I've got nothing to do but feel silly. I'm tired of that."

"Michael and my father and mother all

send their best wishes," said Pam. She bit into the apple. "This is for Mokey, actually. Not for you," she said. "And I'm sure she won't mind if I have a little. Your mother said you couldn't eat an apple, anyway."

"Nothing but tea and toast. And hot, hearty soup," said Ginny. "Yuck."

"My father says," Pam went on, "that you have given yourself a royal concussion. He hopes you've knocked some sense into your head. Because even Mokey can't jump in the dark."

Ginny stared at her. "Even Mokey?"

"Even Mokey." Pam nodded. "He says that Mokey has more sense than the two of us put together. He's one of her biggest fans. And he would like you to let us take care of her for you. Just until you can do it again yourself."

"You're kidding." Ginny shook her head. Then she stopped quickly. It made her dizzy. "You mean in your stable? With Firefly and all those beautiful horses?"

"That's right. And Michael says he will let

me help." Pam grinned. "I never was very interested in caring for horses and ponies. Michael had about given me up as hopeless. But you've had so much fun with Mokey. Taking care of her seems to be such a nice part of it. I feel I've missed a lot."

Ginny sat up straighter in bed. She clasped her arms around her knees. "The doctor said I can't ride for at least four more weeks. Will you exercise her every single day? Even after school starts?"

"Oh, sure," said Pam. "That will be the best part of all."

Ginny stared at her friend. "You mean you've wanted to ride Mokey before this?" she asked.

"For ages."

Ginny leaned her head back against the pillows. The room was tilting a little bit around the edges. "Thank your father very much," she said. "Mokey would love to visit. But will you be sure to tell Michael that she gets three quarts of mixed crushed oats and sweet feed? Morning and night. And that she should have a little grass every day. And that she's very fussy about her water being clean . . ." She stopped. She laughed at herself. "Okay, I guess he knows how."

Pam smiled. "I'll tell him," she promised.

Ginny stood by the window of her room. She watched Pam ride Mokey down the driveway. The pony was striding along cheerfully, as she always did. Ginny saw Pam lean forward. She patted the pony on the shoulder. Ginny sighed in envy.

A light breeze sprang up. A shower of yellow leaves spun down from the maple tree on the lawn. The afternoon smelled of sunlight and falling leaves. There was even a little hint of frost in the air.

Ginny smiled to herself. Then she went back to bed. Her father was right. It had been quite a summer.

About the Author

Jean Slaughter Doty wrote fourteen children's books, including *Can I Get There by Candlelight?*, *The Crumb*, *The Monday Horses*, and *Winter Pony*, the sequel to *Summer Pony*. In her spare time, she bred Welsh ponies, showed hunters, foxhunted, and judged equitation and pony classes at major shows, including the National Horse Show. Her stories about horses and ponies have been treasured by generations of riders—and readers—everywhere.

About the Illustrator

Ruth Sanderson has illustrated over seventy books for children since 1975. She is well known for her lavishly illustrated fairy-tale picture books. In 2003, she won the Texas Bluebonnet Award for *The Golden Mare, the Firebird, and the Magic Ring*. Earlier in her career, she illustrated the first paperback covers for the entire Black Stallion series, as well as a number of chapter-book horse stories. She lives with her family in Easthampton, Massachusetts, and her favorite hobby is horseback riding. Visit her on the Web at www.ruthsanderson.com.